GEORGE
AND
MARTHA

For George and Cecille

The stories in this book were originally published by
Houghton Mifflin Company in *George and Martha*

www.houghtonmifflinbooks.com

Library of Congress Cataloging-in-Publication data is on file.
READER ISBN-13: 978-0-618-96331-7
Printed in Singapore

TWP 10 9 8 7 6 5 4 3 2 1

written and illustrated by

JAMES MARSHALL

HOUGHTON MIFFLIN COMPANY BOSTON

TWO STORIES ABOUT TWO GREAT FRIENDS
STORY NUMBER ONE
SPLIT PEA SOUP

Martha was very fond of making split pea soup. Sometimes she made it all day long. Pots and pots of split pea soup.

Soup's
ON

If there was one thing that George was not fond of, it was split pea soup. As a matter of fact, George hated split pea soup more than anything else in the world. But it was so hard to tell Martha.

One day after George had eaten ten bowls of Martha's soup, he said to himself, "I just can't stand another bowl. Not even another spoonful."

So, while Martha was out in the kitchen, George carefully poured the rest of his soup into his loafers under the table.

"Now she will think I have eaten it."

But Martha was watching from the kitchen.

"How do you expect to walk home with your loafers full of split pea soup?" she asked George.

"Oh dear," said George. "You saw me."

"And why didn't you tell me that you hate my split pea soup?"

"I didn't want to hurt your feelings," said George.

"That's silly," said Martha. "Friends should always tell each other the truth. As a matter of fact, I don't like split pea soup very much myself. I only like to make it. From now on, you'll never have to eat that awful soup again."

"What a relief!" George sighed.

“Would you like some chocolate
chip cookies instead?” asked Martha.
“Oh, that would be lovely,” said George.
“Then you shall have them,” said
his friend.

STORY NUMBER TWO
The Flying Machine

"I'm going to be the first of my species to fly!" said George.

"Then why aren't you flying?" asked Martha. "It seems to me that you are still on the ground."

"You are right," said George. "I don't seem to be going anywhere at all."

"Maybe the basket is too heavy," said Martha.

"Yes," said George, "I think you are right again. Maybe if I climb out, the basket will be lighter."

"Oh dear!" cried George. "Now what have I done? There goes my flying machine!"

"That's all right," said Martha. "I would rather have you down here with me."

JAMES MARSHALL (1942–1992) is one of the most popular and celebrated artists in the field of children's literature. Three of his books were selected as New York Times Best Illustrated Books, and he received a Caldecott Honor Award in 1989 for *Goldilocks and the Three Bears.* With more than seventy-five books to his credit, including the popular George and Martha series, Marshall has earned the admiration and love of countless readers.